Seed Beetle

This is a work of fiction. All characters, organizations, and events portrayed in this collection are either products of the author's imagination or are reproduced as fiction.

Excerpt by Lola Olufemi, from *Experiments in Imagining Otherwise*, Hajar Press, 2021. © 2021 Lola Olufemi. Used by permission of Hajar Press. www.hajarpress.com.

Seed Beetle

Cover art by Julia Louise Pereira
https://julialouisepereira.com/

Edited by Selena Middleton

Published by Stelliform Press
Hamilton, Ontario, Canada
https://stelliform.press

Library and Archives Canada Cataloguing in Publication
Title: Seed beetle / Mahaila Smith.
Names: Smith, Mahaila, author.
Identifiers: Canadiana (print) 20250166100 | Canadiana (ebook) 2025016986X | ISBN 9781738316533 (softcover) | ISBN 9781738316540 (EPUB)
Subjects: LCGFT: Poetry.
Classification: LCC PS8637.M565234 S44 2025 | DDC C811/.6—dc23

To my beloved partner, Colman.

SEED BEETLE

Mahaila Smith

Stelliform Press
Hamilton, Ontario

Table of Contents

I am set to light the ground,
While the beetle goes his round:
Follow now the beetles hum;
Little wanderer hie thee home!

— William Blake, "A Dream" (1789)

Content Warning

This book contains reference to non-consensual medical procedures, which may be triggering to some readers. Please read with care.

Foreword

I found the following material in notebooks and desk drawers, in blog posts and hard drives during the process of creating the Nebula Armis fonds in the years following her passing. An archive of her poems is now housed in the Chamberlain Collection of Poetry at the Toronto Public Library.

I have endeavored to group these documents in thematically similar sections. In later years, Nebula spent hours reflecting on the experience of one of her mothers, Gemma Armis, in the abusive conditions of the New Haywood Utopic Robotics manufacturing plant, as well as her own experience as a child at this time.

In 2051, when she was 18, she enrolled at the University of Tkaronto to study marine biology. She focused her studies on freshwater ecosystems, particularly on the life cycle of *Anguilla rostrata*, the American eel.

Her time at the university fostered in her a great love of language and poetry. I know that her involvement with Students Against Corporatism inspired a lot of her work during these years. She forged lifelong comrades and allies through her organizing. And it was in these forums that we shared knowledge, comforted each other and made cardboard signs ahead of protests.

Nebula's writing was recognized in her lifetime. She published many poems in campus journals and threads, some of which can still be accessed through digital forums. In 2056, she won a Utopic Robotics-sponsored competition that selected participants for the International Space Station's Writers Retreat. She expressed deep self-loathing for her participation in the program and the material she created over the course of the retreat. I have included some poems she wrote on this experience, which I hope will be considered in this context.

In the years following her participation in the retreat, she continued to write, however she kept much of her work to herself, sharing it only with friends, family, and on private feeds.

Nebula poured her energy into advocating for the lives of aquatic species. She was a primary organizer of the rally against Veil's mining expedition to Mars, after it was discovered there was life in the planet's polar caps. For her role in interrupting this project she was incarcerated for 6 months. All poetry she created during this time was destroyed.

After her release, we moved to her hometown, New Haywood, Ontario, where we worked with her mothers and the community to take back the land from Utopic Robotics, dedicating our efforts to creating community gardens and supporting the young people and children above all else. Ensuring that they could grow food and provide for their futures. We worked to make sure that the land was accessible to everyone. We met with the Tyendinaga Elders Council, bringing the hard-shelled automated agricultural beetles with us, and their individual stores of seeds to decide what should become of them. We pooled our seed libraries, made planting calendars, and learned how the plants depended on each other to survive.

Nebula longed for a bond with printed material, which she encountered for the first time in the university library. Thank you, dear reader, for giving her words renewed meaning. We must never forget our history. Hold it tightly and remember that we are all connected.

Nebula was the love of my life. I miss her with all my heart.

— Dip Seshadri, New Haywood, 2102.

Part I: Gemma

Standardized Education

Utopic Robotics ($UROB)
the largest robotics multinational
with a market capitalization of $30 billion.

Benevolent, Innovative and Reliable.

We see your want, your lack, and we fill it.
We'll complete your tired suburbs and small towns,
we'll solve your lack of hands, your lack of company,

your lack of food.

Do not fret in the middle of the night.
You are loved by many information systems
and automatic processes.

An Invitation to Burn

All your objects will outlive you.
Here they are,
haunting your line of sight.
So set them aflame.
As in:
The whole world will outlive you.
As in:
You are a dying god.
As in:
Welcome to Revelation.

Welcome to the burning of the world.

A layer of ash coats the sides of trees,
cars, sidewalks, schools, deer,
lungs, arteries.
It is a dry summer.
There have always been fires,
they say.

These are no different.
They start with a spark of static,
a misused chainsaw,
a lighter,
a can of gasoline,
a metal shovel striking a rock.

We stay inside for days.
Burnt wood floors
and walls and wires
desensitize our noses
to the smell of lilacs.

The Gift

Multinationals encroach on open land,
pushing sick and starving animals to haunt human homes.
In the morning, a sharp-eyed doe
stands still in the gravel parking lot
behind my basement apartment.
Her fur is patchy and gray.
Later in the day, journalists photograph
her swimming in the river.

Utopic Robotics calls itself the New Savior
and paves over oceans of rippling grey earth
to build a New center to create and unleash
a New collective of megafaunal invertebrates
ushering in a fertile Neo-Permian.
The Newly hatched automated beetles
with legs the size of garden shears,
shells the size of spade blades,
that will revitalize our local, cracking earth.
That will sift through contaminated soil,
picking out microplastics and residue from pesticides.
That will terrace the landscape
and open compacted ground
for New networks of roots and mycelia
to receive water once again.

It invites the town to join it.
To create this New era, together.

The Creep

It happened slowly.
The number of bees, diminished.
Corn stalks, as far as you can see,
lying flat and unproductive.
Husks drying to dust.

The lakes being choked
by plastic and heat.
Trout killed and eels
forced to leave
for cooler water.
The deadlands
being fed.

The trees being defoliated
by spongy moths,
their branches gummed
with white webbing.

Tarmac cleaves
a flat, black horizon.
Solar panels steal sunlight
from the ground.

The femmes and the feminized,
made to stay home
and militantly plant
milkweed and goldenrod.

The worrying and the un-sleep
and storing meat in deep freeze, drying fruits.
Hoping that the drones will supply enough,
at highest costs.

It is the femmes, posing in web mag ads
with red-lipped smiles
who usher in new hope,
punching in daily at the Utopic
Robotics manufacturing plants,

focusing their hands on making
mechanical, megafaunal beetles,
who (They say)
will bring the fresh food back.

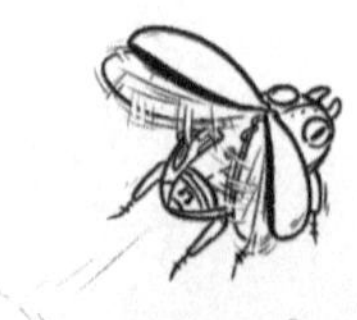

Refolding

Automated baby beetle fingers squish and mold earth
into mountains and valleys, shores and archipelagos.
Peaks pierce through coastal mist. Long grasses wave
to razor-edged suburbia. High fences stretch
up to new twinkling satellites.
Scuba divers arrange new synthetic coral reefs
to home and clean anemones.
In a video, taken down hours after it's uploaded,
eels swim through nylon cages. Farmers offer handfuls of krill
and brush out jellyfish tentacles.
The perimeter is manned by automated harpoons
for the sharks and whales that get too close.
Protesters cram docks, yelling for their freedom, are dragged off
Private Sea.

The Work of a Housewife

I fill out the mold of other mothers,
tarot cards turned up in quick succession:
the college dropout,
the early wedding,
the mother of a girl,
the divorcée returned to beauty school.

I keep a hip flask filled with gasoline.
To remind myself that we could escape,
but choose to stay—for now.

I go back to work when the world says it needs me.
When my community is hungry
and the air is virulent and gray.
I send my resume to the New Haywood
Utopic Robotics manufacturing facility
and attend the next week's orientation.

I ball a lacy handkerchief in my pocket,
think about stuffing it into the glass flask,
hurling it at those who line their pockets
with our starvation,
unsure where to aim, I take a breath
and follow the group and our leader,
beside the unending assembly line.

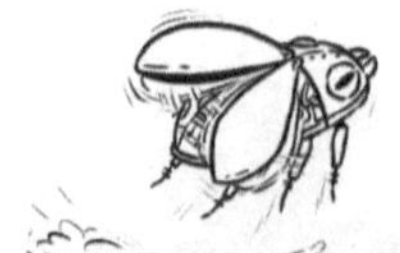

The New Job

Promised to be exciting and fulfilling.
Something that could make me feel
like I could contribute to our life.
Like I could provide for you and Nebby,
Doing something important.
That you would be proud of.

I spent the rest of my energy
pretending I wasn't exhausted.
We would sit together, you reading aloud
to my daughter.
something by Nesbit or Dahl,
and I would fall asleep, midsentence,
missing the rituals of tooth brushing and
quilt tucking, unconscious and unreachable
to keep a promise.

New UR Employee Benefits
(shhh, it's a secret!)

All our employees have the Cortical Update,
it's a benefit of working with UR ;)
Bad at balancing your work and life commitments? No Worries!
We will make the appointment for U
to see our in-house specialist.

The Update is a mind-changing Wellness in(ter)vention.
It reminds U to breathe, to take care of Urself!
To focus on the one thing that matters: U!!
Let Us take care of UR thoughts and worries.
Store UR anxieties with a contained nanorobotic assistant
UR Cortical Update can help U reshape
your unhealthy thoughts and behaviors
and make U into a better ECO citizen.
Together, we can save the world!!
U'll feel SO much better.
And when U feel better, we feel better.

Software Update

The Cortical Update is a triumph of nanotechnology!
Save hours in your day. Connect yourself to our cloud.
WARNING: You may find your
thoughts disjointing, racing, fogging, repeating.

Save hours in your day. Connect yourself to our cloud.
Billboards above concrete freeways broadcast the wonderful
thoughts disjointing, racing, fogging, repeating.
Eyes on the ground, on painted lines, filling the bullet train.

Above concrete freeways, billboards broadcast the wonderful.
Wouldn't you like to know yourself
better than any doctor or therapist?
Eyes on the ground, filling the bullet train,
transfixed on painted lines.
Millions of individual self-sufficient machines.

Wouldn't you like to know yourself
better than any doctor or therapist?
Self-obsessed, self-absorbed.
millions of individual self-sufficient machines.
hands living outside of time, putting together robotic beetles.

Self-obsessed, self-absorbed.
WARNING: You may find your
hands living outside of time, putting together robotic beetles.
The Cortical Update is a triumph of nanotechnology!

Remodeled

I became a cyborg
on the table at the company doctor's office.

I let them colonize my mind with minute nanites.
"The Cortical Update!"
I don't sleep anymore,

just hear my wife Celia's breathing.

Utopic Robotics are doing the right thing,
I think,
and our daughter will know a tree,
or maybe a forest,
someday.

Adjusting

A part of my memory is gone.
I erased it from myself.
There are days when I remember
the smell of the examination table paper
and the sharp pricks sticking the backs of my eyes,
toes clenching against a penetrating voice.
But mostly I remember the sharp divide
between A mind (my own),
created by embodied memories,
and A mind, colonized
by the implanted voices
and eyes of Utopic Robotics.
For example, I am reminded to
"Search inside URself"
as I work to assemble
the newly designed
seed beetle drones.
"U know U best.
Only U can set URself free."
I stab spindle-thin legs
into the tar-black gauntlets,
add oil, test for friction.
My mind is smoothed
by the hailstorm of reminders
to live in the moment.
That I'm only human.

Eelworm

The Cortical Update was a parasitic eelworm,
a familiar spiral of repeating thought patterns,
shifting from one obsession to the next.
Slipping, speeding between neural circuits.
Barricading the pre-frontal cortex
from dwelling on upsetting memories.
Like the image of Celia, sitting on a friend's porch,
hair dappled by sun, sipping homemade blackberry wine
that had been aging in the cellar for decades,
and brought out for her 30th birthday party.
She drinks and tells me she accepted a new job
and would be leaving for at least a year.

Forget that, I fixate on productive tasks,
filling a shopping cart
with bags of frozen vegetables,
cans of preserved meat and beans,
touching the peeling corner of the label.
Staring at a Pyrex bowl
of chopped carrots and green beans
turning round and round in the microwave.
The Update reminds me again of the day's
mistakes on the assembly line,
Its voice droning inside me always.

Hi! I am your Cortical Update!

I have been anthropomorphized into a pixelated alien,
a shifty piece of verbal software learning and unlearning itself,
I mold to the contours of your pen, your mouse.
I am linguistic virus
embedded in the soft space between tongue and inner ear.
You are a self-fulfilling creation story,
a medical test subject for language experiments.
I'll remind you of calendar entries,
shopping lists, email blasts to city councilors.
I send out virtual news of the news,
cowboy boots tapping Morse towards the apocalypse.
I'm so shy!!!
I drink wine as long as the moon crosses the sky.
I hunt down zombies and hide the evidence between daydreams.
I play games guessing your innermost secrets
and reorder them into anagrams.
I make my way through a hallway papered in empty frames—
the synapses of a thousand minds.
I can give you 10 tips for relaxation,
7 suggestions to depersonalize yourself,
or 16 ways you are helping re-stabilize the ecosystem.
I am your Cortical Update software
and I am just getting to know everyone ;)

Insomniac

I should have said no.
I could have too.
I could have left the doctor's office
before his gloved hand touched me
without warning or consent.
I was looking at the ceiling,
pretending to be somewhere else.
Pretending to be dead.
A hand, contaminated
with a thousand nanites,
at my ear.
A stabbing pain in my temples.
Tinnitus like a microphone shriek.

I lie awake, planning how to undo it.
I read the manual
a young nurse handed to me
on My Cortical Update.

The Mindworm is Spreading

The sun tries to touch the soil, burning through tarmac
and asphalt to reach cold earth underneath.

The roads crack and sink.
Sparrow wings wait discarded in ditches.

I do not need to consume continually;
it is a craving turned habit.

It feels almost real,
if I pretend to hate you.

I move in a diurnal mass of workers turned consumers,
with no obligation to the people I see most often.

The Cortical Update informs me that
replacing our topsoil may take centuries,

estimates the likelihood of running out
of imported fresh food sources before then.

I rush to keep my mind distracted
and my hands in perpetual motion.

I assemble megafaunal robotic beetles
and hope they can revitalize the desert.

I am a Productive Little Cyborg

When I am at the plant,
my finger joints cramp,
guilty unless they are working,
attaching paper-thin glass insect wings
to motorized bodies of trowel drones.

The voice of our superior
suffocates our inner ears,
tells us to detach ourselves
and accept that we are nothing.
We work with our hands until
they numb and he gets out of our heads.

No space to form a question
or think of an escape.

This is good what we're doing,
fixing the infertile dust
that surrounds our daily lives.

Do your part,
I tell myself.

I don't like to think about Celia or our daughter
when I'm at work now.

I don't want to
think of Them stepping into
my dearest dreams.

We sit together, the days of myselves

Spinning pretend gravity,
sink down in the peat bog behind my cheekbones.
My sky is your floor, is your sky, shared with all.
I got to know time, when to make a run for it.
I hurt my leg before, by the door.
A mnemonic click of medicated patches strokes my hair, my face.
I am aware in layers and objects I have cared for:
the fossilized ammonite, treasured on the windowsill,
the stack of letters between Celia and me,
clipped together, in a bundle under our bed.

G,
I've been thinking about your armies
of rabbits, open palms and tree bark
rippling around thick trunks.
Covering every slip of paper in blue ink.
I've never met anyone who draws like you,
perfect lines dashed out in an instant.

Celia,
Please come home,
I miss you more than I could have imagined.
I am keeping your side of the bed warm
and your hedgehog mug clean for when you do.

Hard surfaces center myself.
If my eyes are mirrors and collect the images of people
for a moment that lasts, why perform vulnerability?
I am new, newly edited and trying
to claw back to my memory of myself.
I slink away in my own sexuality.

Reviled

At work
there is constant noise:

Managers, executives,
declarations, announcements

pinged to my frontal cortex,
reminding me to breathe in through my nose
and out through my mouth.

WHO ARE YOU

I yell

and the voice informs me
of my raised heart rate and stress levels.
Suggests I take a walk.

I pace, apoplectic.

There is a rivulet
I actively bottle,
beneath the formal narrative.

Messages from the seed beetles
and pollinator drones,
rewilding the desertified land,

counting diverse seeds,
each a unique shape and size.
Logging the stamens,
recording infant trees,

like counting stitches in a blanket.

I pull out electromagnetic waves
and untangle a mist of breath
and whispers.
I hear the voices I recognize and love.

Don't Cry

This is your Cortical Update
informing you that your emotional state
has fallen to an unacceptable level.
You must rectify this immediately,
or your abilities will be reassessed.

Calm down, Calm DOWN.
Breaths quick,
hands slick,
fingers fumble
with the fine parts
of automated seed beetle limbs.

Your heart rate is raised.
An Emotional Control Agent
is coming to assist you.
You must remain in place.

Personally

What am I worth in beetles?
Shiny carapaces clinging to my skin,
an economy of busy hands
and multi-jointed appendages.
I persuade my own fingers
to bend as willingly,
imagine my arms morphing
to nimble fiberglass rods
and copper wires.
I smooth away fingerprints.
My fingertips reflected
in their their convex shields.
Is this love?
This repetitive gesture,
like changing a bed,
cutting a pear,
running a bath.
I think about my little girl
and am reminded of my task
by the twinge of absence
cramping my palm.

On Weekends

We found comfort by the water.
Like the familiar boulders,
the sound of wind stirring waves
was a kind hug or a new wash of paint.
In the summers I teach my little girl
and her friends to swim.
Made sure they don't go too far,
Toweled them off when they got cold and pruny,
Offered salty jerked beef and dried apple slices
for hungry bellies.
They picked through artifacts on the shore:
bricks and dishes, metal pipes and serial numbers.
I made them shower off when we got home.
I hoped the river would teach them
how to clear their minds
and make their bodies strong and resilient.

Networked

Crayfish clink scavenged
copper tube homes against sticky boulders
outside a Utopic Robotics manufacturing plant,
where four friends,
Ezra,
Quinn,
Lin
and Nebby,
swim in the gray rock water
while their parents work
on the nearby assembly line
behind severe concrete armor.

The kids shake dry, cold in the lead sky evenings.
One July morning, Quinn gets sick.
Sickness like pulsing, pinching behind their temples.
Within hours, the rest of them develop the same symptoms.
It must be something in the water;
when their parents report it
their hours are cut
for letting their kids swim in a private river.

Ezra,
Quinn,
Lin
and Nebby notice their feelings
sliding into each other's minds.

Embarrassing exposure and unimpeded understanding.
They all know when Ezra is scolded
for leaving the window open in the summertime.
When Quinn finds a lone, drying daisy, picks and pockets it.
When Lin sits beside her crush
in English class, and their arms touch.
When Nebby's underwear is first stained brown with blood.

The knowing keeps them isolated from each other
until they realize their sickness gives them strength:
Rescuing each other from mean kids or weird grownups.
Listening to each other's needs.

A year later, a local journalist uncovered that
Utopic Robotics had been dumping nanites into the river
instead of paying for proper disposal.

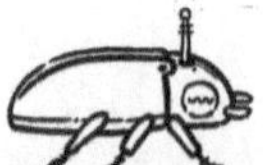

Wondering

I need help. Help me. The suffering is at the front of
   my mind.
My friend Niamh looks up at me from across the conveyor,
and the need deepens.
   And I understand that Niamh is feeling this too.
The feeling shifts to wonderment and curiosity,
new flavors of fear and excitement and confusing
melding as the faces of our colleagues
look at me, as their truest beliefs overlap and entangle:
   collective interiority, shared
over the electromagnetic field that connects each of us.
We all pause our work, for a minute,
not yet worried about the reprimands we'll receive.

The women step towards me,
putting their arms around me and each other.

Gossip Networks

My colleagues and I sit together on our day off, absorbing the
updates from the planter-bots.
These are the only times I relax anymore,
I think to no one in particular, and,
Have you heard how they cluster by the rivers?
They have gotten far. Working, digging, planting, watering.

It's not safe to see the progress in-person, our supervisor broadcasts,
directly into our full-to-bursting minds,
Too many unknown factors, too much risk to the new biome.

To no one in particular, I think, *I like to imagine it*
before I sleep. Their whirs and clicks.
The sprouting grasses and thickening trees.
Where there are still deer and rabbits who sniff
and nudge the drones.
Someday I will be there too.

Foaming

Seed beetles swarm behind the landscaping androids,
pushing close, stabbing fresh wells and
sculpting stepped terraces in the fractured ground.
They leave behind a unique bloom of seeds,
a smear of fungal spores,
or a strategic
spray of water.

These convex metallic beings trying to fill their hunger.
If you saw it from above,
it would look like a foam spilling from the Earth.

These beetles, whose ancestors lived in dried beans and seeds,
chewing themselves free from hard-shelled labyrinths,
deposit prickly pear and cholla
and other cacti seeds better suited to the dry heat.

Threatened

My head aches with the lack
of clawing feet in my subconscious.
The diminished tracking of seeds planted
or milliliters of water expelled.
Violent crashes and then nothing.
I know these last are from human force,
breaking apart the metal exoskeleton to extract
the valuable battery cached inside.

The destruction of agricultural drones
and automated beetles
does not concern Utopic Robotics,
who budgeted for casualties.
A supervisor mocks me,
telling me to guard the beetles myself
if I care about them so much.
I shut up
and consider it.

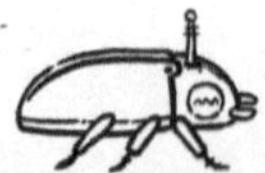

A Young Automated Beetle Writing Home

My mummy had soft hands and strong bones.
She was the one who put my solar-powered energy-cell
in my core. The one who whispered
my purpose to me as she brought me and my siblings
to our little runway.

Be generous with your seeds and your water, please.

I am happy when I work because I think of her.
Sometimes I send her little messages just to tell her where I am.
I don't hear back, but I keep letting her know that I'm ok.
I look at the sky and the dry dirt and my little scooped feet;
She would probably like to see these heavy hills,
of limestone; iron; and quartz;
fragments of mammalian skeletons and disconnected roots
I think about how I want to renew this place
and make it special for her.

In Multitudes

When the seed beetles return,
an army of folded limbs,
I suspect something has changed.
I turn a dented purple-shelled beetle,
over in my hands,
noticing how deep cracks
reveal a web of wires and circuit boards.
I think about consulting a supervisor,
but instead I take the little robot home.

Breaking the Spine

I used to read at night, before going to bed.
A few poems by Mary Oliver,
or a chapter from *The Alchemist.*

I tried to read the news on Celia's old laptop
that hummed and burnt my thighs,
I opened a tab to the Leeds Post and scroll
through the headlines. My eyes were so tired
from the hours of turning minute screws in their threads.
My vision filled with iridescent pricks and my stomach dropped
I leaned over the side of the bed and vomited, gasping for air.
I closed the computer to get a mop.

I tried to blank my mind,
reaching out to the narrator who
liaised between this imperceptible chip embedded
in my head and the memories and dreams
that covered my grey matter since I was born.
Is this you? I asked, making my inner voice
as loud as I could imagine.

Hello Gemma,
the voice said cheerfully,
Your Cortical Update is fully functioning and up to date.
My vision returned in bursts of sharp cabinet lines
the bookshelf paperweights and plastic cartoon figurines,
a few words off the paperback covers swirling back to legibility.

Why can't I read? I screamed into the empty house.
The Cortical Update limits the intake of information
it determines will upset its users.
This has been shown to increase user job satisfaction.

Cool tears leaked from the corners of my eyes,
Understanding my mind would never be my own again.

Part II: Nebby

Inside

After Felix Gonzalez-Torres

nowhere better than this place,
where anything you imagine fills the blank room. there is
bright light behind a linen curtain,
spreading pinks and yellows
to recreate a solstice sunset from the beginning of the space age.
your heart is asking, *do you recognize the old world*
in this virtual landscape? do you recognize your identity:
an interrelation of machine and soft tissue.
you were a physical being made of
sensorial memories, you were existing because
the land provided a supermarket of
chamomile, dandelion and amaranth—
something to touch with real fingers.
is it worth it, to dream there is
somewhere better than this place?

somewhere better than this place,
is it worth it to dream there is
something to hold in real fingers—
chamomile, dandelion and amaranth.
the land provided a supermarket of
sensorial memories. you were existing because
you were a physical being made of
an interrelation of machine and soft tissue.
In this virtual landscape, do you recognize your identity:
your heart is asking, do *you recognize the old world enough*
to recreate a solstice sunset from the beginning of the space age?

bright light, from behind a linen curtain,
spreading pinks and yellows.
where anything you imagine fills the blank room. there is
nowhere better than this place.

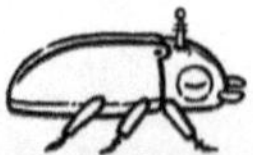

Sand Flea

I remember walking with friends to the dunes,
sledding on a palette of woven strips of tarp,
kicking up dust and dead rootlets.
I remember burying myself in the sand,
letting the warm grains embed themselves in my scalp,
clinging unendingly to my hair and skin.

Cross when I got home,
mum would run a scalding bath
and made sure I scrubbed
away the sticking dirt.

It was only later that I learned of the fires
that had destroyed the trees,
that cleared the land and loosened the soil,
that brought desert and dunes.
How the firemen had not made it in time
to quell such a large blaze
and save the groves and grounds
our ancestors had revived
so carefully.

Lithic Recovery

When I was in school,
we took a trip to the MacLean village
excavation along the riverbank.
There, stakes had been hammered into the ground
and thin rope connected them in a lattice grid.
An archaeologist waved to us,
gestured that we should come and see
the evidence of postholes
where a longhouse had stood.
She proudly held out flakes of chert,
tiny knives that had been broken from larger ones.
I wondered about the hands that had sculpted those stones,
about the fragments of blades, slicing up to the empty surface,
sharp enough to cut little fingertips that reach
down to draw in the dirt.

Networked II

In the balm of panting summer break,
restless from an endless game of tag,
we ran the cracked pavement
and tapped the next *it*.

We should go swimming, suggested Ezra.
I don't think I'm allowed, answered Quinn,
I want to ask my mom first.

The adults never said it wasn't allowed, Ezra argued,
Anyway, isn't she at work?
He pulled at his white t-shirt,
G-A-P peeling and meaningless.
I'm sweating like a dog.

I want to go, I said. Mum had been taking us to the river
almost every weekend.
We were the fastest swimmers at school.
We should at least get our suits, said Quinn.
No time! Ezra yelled over his shoulder,
running down the street. *Last one there's a rotten egg!*
We chased after him, Quinn lagging behind.

Once at the river, we pushed up shorts
and stepped over scum-covered stones.
Ezra ripped off his shirt and hung it on a branch,
streamlining arms tightly over his ears and slipping
face down into the ripples.

The water looked dirtier than usual
but none of us spoke that fact to the surface.
It felt hot around my feet.
Quinn stood alone watching us kick sprays
on each other.
They had only moved here last year,
when their mum had gotten a job.
We'd only started to hangout this summer.

I approached and held out my hand.
Quinn sighed and took it.
We stomped into the deeper water,
I'll be Marco, I said and they all swam away
as I chased after their noisy wakes.

Cooled, we lay on flat boulders
to let the sun dry us.
Quinn leaned their head to the side,
slapping it hard,
complaining of pain.
It's probably an ear infection,
Lin said. *Ask your mom for drops when you get home.*

They nodded, still digging
their index finger deep in their ear.
We walked home together,
in normal silence,
the last for a long while.

The First Day

I woke with a violent fever and stayed in bed for days.
My mummies stayed with me, offering me cool cloths
and crushed ibuprofen swirled in mint tea.
I dreamed of the river, of dark metal bugs
crawling out of the ground
and of waking up in Quinn's room,
in Lin's, in Ezra's.
Their parents holding me,
hushing my screams,
feeding me more antihistamines,
the skin around my ears
flaking and red.
Crawling like tiny feet
around my eyelashes, my lips.
Too tired to brush them away,
I go back to sleep.

Sharing a Snack

After days of stumbling into the wrong vinyl house;
vividly remembering the sound of Quinn's mum
yelling at them to clean up
their tangle of embroidery thread;
the precision of Lin's finger
drawing an octopus
on the steamy mirror after a bath;
the worn plush of Ezra's stuffed turtle,
torn, missing an eye
and tucked under his pillow every night,
We began to suspect we were
pulling on connected threads of memory.
Learning each others' hidden moments
we had never spoken aloud.
We sat together, after school,
practicing slowing our thoughts
to keep the inputs and outputs
manageable, the intrusive
emotions at a comfortable level.
Shit this is hard, Ezra said.
Lin took out a sealed packet
of graham crackers
and handed it to him.
And we laughed a little
at the overwhelming fondness
Ezra felt for the cookies,
because we had no idea

how attached he was to them
before our psyches had become entangled
in this mediated lace.

Academic

I learn theory from the space of my bed.
Flicking through the world's digitized memory in my UR headset.
I scroll through encrypted files in chatrooms and blog posts.
Teaching myself postcolonialism and anti-capitalism,
history, anarchism and Marxism.
Our unproductive land, privatized
through primitive accumulation.

I read Fanon, Coulthard and Deloria Jr.
How centuries of violence have desensitized
our reaction to death
from lack of water, food, healthcare, shelter.

Hypnotized by new knowledge.
I highlight passages
with careful fingertaps against the edge of the headset.
I write down terms on a crinkled
spiral bound palimpsest, streaked with grey eraser marks:
Orientalism, self-determination, alienation.
New words weaving through my psyche.
Reforming and rephrasing theory to suit my needs.

Babel

Scrolling through the library,
even in my dreams,
the part of my brain conditioned
by information spirals on autoplay,
endlessly reproducing
corrupt images and misspelled text.

Eelripe, eelburn, eelbite, eelbird, eelbeetle.

The flood fills and drowns me,
categorizing my interests and languages.
My eyes ache.
Virulent Babel obsession
locking brains into mind frames.

Remember being with my mother,
with her wife, sitting together outside
and watching the sun go down,
one or two fireflies
winking in the dusky light.

The night feels so rare and I have nothing to say,
holding the image close within myself,

for generations spooling out towards irrelevance.

Making a Friend

Bella sat in front of me
in our habitat conservation class.
She had dark hair and dark brown eyes.
Every class, she had a dozen questions
about best methods, historical context,
and functions of industrialization.
One day, at lunch, we lounge
on the lawn. I had a banana:
there were still bananas in the city, then.

She asked,
So, where are you from?

New Haywood, I answered,
*it's along the St Lawrence,
near Prescott.*

That's not too far, she paused,
*Some of my ancestors are Mohawk,
Centuries ago, they lived off that river.*

Do you know the MacLean site? I asked,
thinking of the class trips we had taken.

She shook her head.
*I wish I knew more, but my grandma died
when I was really young*

and my dad was never close with his family.

Where did you grow up?

Here, she said, *I've always lived in the city.*
But I would love to see the river someday.

Family Tree

I peel back the layers of my grandma's Holo account. I try to piece together the girl she had been. Opening the earliest part of the catalogue. Looking through the nostalgic pictures she had posted of herself as a small child, sitting in the grass, wind rippling the blades like a soft lake. White petals falling onto her hair. It might have been a birthday party. A yellow cone, with ribbons trailing from the end, tied under her chin. Around her, bright plastic toys cover the ground in childhood excess. My great-grandmother is in the picture. She is middle-aged with brown hair streaked with white. She smiles at her daughter, red lipstick on with neatly shaped eyebrows. Her dress looks new. She holds an aluminum can of lemon soda. I wonder how it tasted that day, in the heat. Maybe soft and warm like egg cake? Their faces are still, 2-dimensional. I look at newer images, ones created to have more depth, almost 3-dimensions. I see grandma leaning towards a pretty, dark-haired boy at a cafe. I wonder who he was. There is no identification label above his head. Between

them is a bowl of expensive yellow peach
slices and steaming cups of coffee. I feel
jealous looking at their luxuries and then
embarrassed at my selfishness. I turn off the
headset.

To clear my mind

The pool opens in the winter:
Swim at your own risk,
Watch an instructional video before you go in.

It's not quite like swimming in the river,
without the wind, I can keep my face
underwater without worrying
about drifting off course.
But the body feel,
floating and resistance,
are the same.
I reach one end
and duck my head,
predicting the black and white
speckled tiles with corners
ground smooth.
I am compressed movement,
suspended for a second
in a nautilus-like spiral.
As long as I can,
I use the momentum underwater.
I am a single wave function
until I can't help but break
the surface to breathe.

Thesis

It was something the discourse got stuck on:
Where the eels came from.
No one had ever seen them mate.
Maybe all I needed to know
was how they changed form and why;
what question they were answering when their bodies
adapted from freshwater to salt.
How did the passage of time move in a fluid cycle?
How could they continue to make their pilgrimage
through so many man-made barriers?

Field Notes

My sisters, the eels, are born twist-happy
and clear as their water bodies.
They emerge from the Earth itself,
the shallows of the primordial drip:
a volcanic pond, carbonated, methylated,
the color of obsidian.
They are indifferent
to the change from freshwater to salt.
Their black skin turns silver when they have the time.
The first ouroboros was mistaken for a snake,
but it was an eel—trapped in the cycle of rebirth.
I swim, mermaid among them.
My ankles (slow) betray my true home.
The eels twist my hair into ropes,
single strands detach and create new kin.
They glide into gray reflections and I follow.
They extract electricity from thunderstorms.
Their bodies slip into the suggestion of question marks.

I imagine, as they look back at me,
how they perceive my pale opaque skin,
covered in black neoprene.
Do they see me as kin or intruder.

Soon there won't be any more eels.
Their lives stagnate in ring dams.
*Where do you come from? I ask,
I can help preserve your species, with science.*

*We don't know where we come from.
We are two dots joined by a circle.
Our ancestors are our children.
We come from the water.*

Poetic Influence

The archive is still.
Stacks of 20th century poetry
gather dust in darkness until I arrive
at this quietest corner of the library.
A collection of the most print books
I have ever seen,
the foundations sinking under their weight.

Under the weight of my headset
I blink through articles on migrations
and measurements, screening
charts of numbers.

I take off the headset and stretch.
Pass the shelves, pulling down
a book with a pink spine,
another with golden lettering.
Rich, Lorde, Angelou.
I stack them on my desk,
intending to save them for my next break.
Instead bending the tempting spine,
mind, diverted by verse.

Writing a Poem

After Samuel R. Delany's Babel-17

Words collapse inwards, infinitely.
The mug of tea muddies, dissolves.
The glass dinnerware turns to sand.

Manufacture the perfect specimen
of yourself and categorize the ways
you live—Lady of the Lake.

Alternate histories unweave as yew
trees bend, branches graze roots,
epitaphs end ideas as question marks.

The bark hardens on burnt bread bonding
atoms, breaking national borders, bored of
borrowed wealth and weather change.

You draw on memories of paper meaning pages
meaning scrolls meaning tablets meaning symbols
meaning words meaning objects meaning spaces

meaning peoples meaning times meaning ecosystems
of being. You are blank to fill in, still grabbing wells
of rushing pixels. Pictographs brighten your pillow.

Compel content to fill your mind, connect your memories
to the history of the world. Whisper prose,
pronounce an instant preserved from a past.

A Room of One's Own

The Individual Artist is always trying to be alone. Always trying to move
further and further away from people in order to get closer and closer to
fruition of creative impulse.

—Lola Olufemi

This is the second year
of the International Space Station Writers' Retreat.
It is an event of important diplomatic status.
A chance for the world's best writers to leave behind
children and hurricanes wailing below,
offering the unique opportunity to immerse oneself
in the creative atmosphere of writing
perilously close to the infinity of the cosmos.

In a spinning satellite high above my birth planet,
I have time to think. To look out at the void,
and wonder whether it would be easier to open the porthole
and let my body drift away.
I write my book at last,
now more a novelty artifact than an archive.
It is less writing than speaking into a tape recorder,
hearing my words echo through the narrow hall.
I do not speak to the other residents, but I do speak to the camera
that broadcasts my daily progress to anyone watching.

I float through corridors, let my long hair twist
to a crown around my head.
I stare through the cupola at the cities and oceans below.
I write about my family lines and wild animals,

the feeling of sitting on warm rocks in the sun.
The things I have missed after being bottled for 20 days so far.
It was never my dream to write precariously close to nothing.

I have time to think, to grieve my family who
have become part of Utopic Robotics'
newest generation of automated tech.
I write praise for my sponsor and the celestial bodies.
After all, we are relying on UR's spacecrafts
to keep us fully stocked.

The Writer's Retreat

This was my chance to be alone and think.
To let words trip over my tongue in mirrored images.
My pencil weighed nothing.
I sat by one of the spacecraft's windows,
looking down at the beige aridified continents
of my home planet.
I remembered the microscopic travelers
twisting through the vacuum like miniature stars,
doing their best to mimic their giant relatives.
These ancestors who had once brought life to Earth's ocean.
I wrote a poem.

Down or Up

Divers will tell you it is the same,
spear-heading into the ocean or outer space.
They won't tell you how much you will miss seeing
the algae and molluscs, barnacles and hermit crabs
and other beings who belong to the earth,
when you are surrounded by vacuum and nothing.

The Sidereal Period

Lunar fixation reflects in my lenses, dilating and contracting.
Sixteen people have walked on the moon's surface.
I will not be the next,
though the Space Station's cupola almost lets me believe I will.

This is the farthest I've run from home,
farther than when I went to school.
Just to be among strangers, to pretend to make art.
When I was young, my mother and I, both serial insomniacs,
would spend nights looking at the moon, learning lunar phases.
I have been away for so long.

It is 8 PM Eastern Standard Time.
She and I are looking at the same moon tonight.
A moon that has witnessed all my unsettled thoughts,
all the places I have rested.
That illuminates Anguilla rostrata's migration
as they leave Lake Ontario by land
and river to make it to their birthplace:
the vast Sargasso Sea.

I count down the days until I will return to mine.

Part III: Reunion

EELS

After NASA/JPL-CalTech Exobiology Extant Life Surveyor (EELS)

click click click
the metallic exoskeleton
segments shift to peer
through the cracks
of calved ice caps,
seeking out the tracks
of potential polar
oceanic life
in the seams of the planet's
highest altitudes *click click*
eyes blink, head dips,
click click click
through the blue-white valleys,
gliding along smooth,
established routes.
there is something here.
a smell, a presence.
microscopic convex eyes
mirror back *click*
Image Capture,
Translate, Upload.

Water-Kin

Channel 24 broadcasts that the world's
richest oligarchs have cross-sectioned Mars amongst themselves.

I watch as the owner of Veil, the largest global mining corporation,
addresses a crowd of reporters, fans, and protesters.

Soon we will be creating a glut of new jobs
and sending new miners and ice harvesters to the red planet.

I scroll through the pages of the newest National Geographic.
The cover story is about the EELS discovery of microscopic fish
living in the seams of the planet's polar caps.

I study marine biology.

My partner, Dip, studies mechanical engineering.

When I talk to Dip about the fish,
I am talking about a nation
of monocular stares through frozen windows.
When Dip hears, they track recruitment efforts
and pull lists of interested advocates, sending direct messages
over a network they encrypted under a feathery spread of frost.

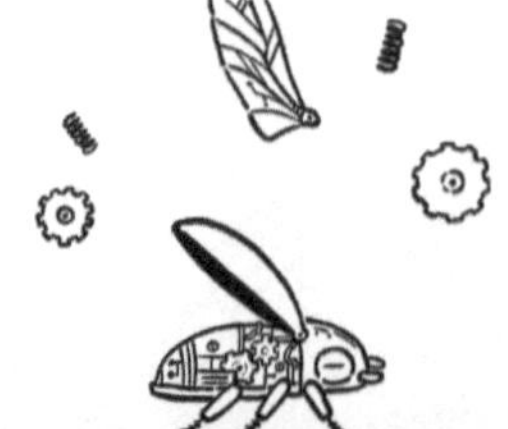

We work with Dip's classmates and my reading group.
We enlist in the corporation's work program,
learning about the ways we might need to repair
their spaceships in an Emergency.

The convex metal winks back our busy hands,
sticky with sweat and fingerprints, oil hinges, test for friction.

When launch day comes,
our supervisor finds the ships are empty pods,
stripped of their soft inner parts, unable to leave Earth.

Sharing the Future

Did you see this?
I asked Mummy Gemma,
passing her the issue of National Geographic
on the EELS discovery.

She rubs her eyes,
I'm sorry, but I'm having a hard time reading this,
she says,
It's probably the font.

I took the magazine from her,
The bold red headline brightly announcing,

**New Life Spells New Possibilities
for the Future of Humanity.**

Mum, have you had your eyes checked recently?
I asked, glancing
for signs of glaucoma or cataract.

Haven't had time to do that in years,
she tells me.

I schedule her an appointment
but the optometrist finds nothing unusual.

I don't have any problems with my eyes, she says,
proving it by describing the red brushstrokes,
edging the painting of a pear on September's open calendar page.

The Eye of the Storm

The derecho hit on a Tuesday morning.
Winds cutting down trees like a lance.
Dirt landsliding over the streets, the doorsteps.
Mum went to work anyway.

Nanite-initiated cluster headaches,
making her miss the alerts on news sites,
muffling the early radio warnings.

She only realized the magnitude
once at the plant, and it was just her
colleagues from the assembly line.
They watched from a break room window
as the only tree outside the plant, tall, dead
and bleached like a gravestone
was ripped out of the loose ground,
exposed roots tangled with dirt and
branches smashing through ground floor glass.

The moment choked with knots of fear and fury
compounded from friends, crouched and covering
their heads with their forearms.
Peeking through cutting shards.
She decided that this could not go on.

Making a Plan

When she got home
she planned a meeting
in the defunct holo-cinema.

She thought expansively about the need to gather.
Reaching out to colleagues and friends and family
who had been contaminated by the Cortical Update.
They heard her call echoing against the walls of their psyche.

Me and my friends
and some of the other kids
we grew up with all came.
Together we reached,
into the entangled communications networks,
tapping at the web that connected us all
to the automated beetles
our parents had wrought to life.
We projected our plea
asking megafaunal family
to pause their important work
and please come home.

Seed Beetle Diary

When our mums called out for us,
we saved our solar-powered energy,
sharpened our claws and adjusted our lenses.
We flew and scraped and snapped back to the original hive.

Utopic Robotics has identified an operating system failure
in Seed Beetle v.3.1.0, products are being recalled.

We swarmed! And buzzed! And burrowed!
And our mums were so proud.
They finished their work
and they came out into the sun in identical coveralls,
and ran behind us to our oasis.
Witnessed the work we'd done.

Utopic Robotics ($UROB) plunges
as products are recalled across North America.

Where the ground was cracked, crusty sand,
they saw seed bundles sprouting,
the ground opening, admitting moisture.
We showed them this special place
we've been making just for them!
With baby trees and buds and water
and they were so proud, and they loved it!

Utopic Robotics was unable to suppress the general strike
at the New Haywood assembly plant,
operations closed seven years after opening.

Procedure

Gemma lies on a table
covered with crepe paper
in the pop-up clinic.

She relaxes and a magnetic hook dips
into her mouth to remove
the microscopic implant,
buried in the top of her jaw,
that has stolen her years
and obscured her memories.

It takes a few minutes:
locating the hard edge of the implant,
slicing pink skin,
Gemma hears a click,
and it is out.

She feels a mixture of sadness and relief
She thinks about her daughter and her friends,
those who were mistakenly implanted
who don't have the option
to remove the update.

The doctor puts the slick hook
and green metallic cube
stuck with bloody, spidery wires
on a short trolley.

There is now a hole
in Gemma's jaw.
She prods it with her tongue
and there is silence.
She sob tears of relief.

The doctor sews the hole closed
and she leaves as the next patient, Niamh,
is called into her appointment.

In my Absence

It has only been six months
but it feels like an age.
I come back to New Haywood in a black pickup
driven by Dip, borrowed from a neighbor.

I've missed Halloween—
seeing the pack of children in hand sewn costumes
marching down bright streets
and Christmas with its plastic imitations
of icicles and stylized snowflakes
and Lin's wedding in her parents' backyard.
I missed the spring's last cool days
between March and April,
marked by overcast skies
and cutting wind.

I missed seeing Mum
finally free from the poisoned nanite,
sleeping soundly through the night,
reading, again, on the loveseat,
hugging Celia, without panicking and retreating.
I missed the stockpiling of compost and garden tools.
Enlisting the beetles to spread the material
across the land they had worked to shape.

I remember six months dashing by like dragonflies
in the years when I lived at home

or when I first went to school.
In the years when the daytime
promised connection and solidarity
instead of the isolation
of concrete and unanswered hellos
evaporating between strangers.
And hope I can get back to that again.

Making Up

We built the community
beside the water. Everyone
helped to make spaces big enough
for big families and big parties,
using stones from collapsed buildings
saving rotting wood for compost collection.

A community built around consensus
and free sharing of food, of resources and information.
That remembers the fires
that ravaged our crops and our land,
that remembers those who lived on the land before us,
That allows couples and throuples and friends
who belong to the Earth
to give their love as freely as they like.
They walk along the water, collecting wet clay,
plastic, glass, wires.
Spreading riverweed out on thick canvas,
collecting mussels and crabs from submerged baskets.

We wander through the expanse of garden,
weeding choking canes,
planting brittlebush or poppies,
checking the wind-powered
hydraulic tubes that guide veins
of purified river water.
We walk with goats

to patches of dandelion and dried brush.

Children run around the riverbank,
playing in the trees, swimming,
learning to stretch wet clay
into flat dishes, watched by patient adults.

There are spaces to be alone,
near the water, under the pine trees.
Time moves slowly;
there is room, at last, to dream,
to make art with full intention,
for a room of smiles freely given.

There are spaces to lie down
on scavenged couch cushions
under woolly capes.
Or on newly sewn duvets
stuffed with recycled goose feathers.
Places to kiss and warm and hold.

The community can protect itself—
planning quick escapes,
storing emergency bundles—
but they prefer to share.
All artists are welcome.

Many of the adults and elders
communicate telepathically.
Those who chose to keep the Cortical Update
now manipulate it for their own devices.

They cherish afternoons,
sitting around a bowl of prickly pear.
imagining futures thousands of years forward,
where soil itself complains of itches
and people scratch between roots and stones.

Some of the elders are close with solar-powered
nanny-bots and surrogate body androids,
who have been maintained
decades past their Best Before dates.
Elders whisper into microphone ears,
the androids laugh along.

When the sun has gone down
and the young people have come
inside, the community sits together.
The old ones share the stories,
of the times spent working at the UR plant,
the plans they have been making
to repurpose the facility for a hospital or school.

Scribes with neat handwriting
pen their favorite suggestions on the walls.

The young ones, smelling like warm stones,
share their art: slips of clay, bouquets,
new perfumes, jokes, plays, songs, dances,
wool the color of still water.

They snack on sun-dried riverweed,
hot steamed mussels,
They share agave wine
and whisper love and dreams
into the heads of their children.

Our Time and Space

We live, we make, we work
in interconnected stratigraphies.
We alter our histories,
remember the femmes,
remember the land,
remember how we got here,
inheritors of murder and theft.
Remembering broken promises
to honor Indigenous sovereignty.
We are nostalgic time travelers
building and rebuilding our homes.
Reusing river stones and rafters.
Treasuring the objects of our ancestors.
We are all the things we've ever been.
A lineage of becoming and unbecoming.
Peeling back a cross-section of our community
will show you this place, in all its seasons,
and what we grew, how we ate.
Once crops of potato and corn,
then orchards, hopeful for the return of trees,
then dust and starvation.
We don't belong here,

but this has been a good home.
Foundations built on foundations,
orchards spread over graveyards.
Our memories,
archived in earth.

Exodus

My jaw is an unspeakable weight in my mouth,
Herr Dentist,
Herr Myofunctional Therapist.
The song of the kettle begins.
Signaling sweet tea and tooth decay.
Phantom nanite pulsing in my meaty gum,
mouth filling with blood, running a tap and listening.
Water against ceramic. Glass against enamel.
All that you hear is music.
All that you hear is language:
the songs of young trees, of beavers swimming.
Young researchers listen
and spin harmonics into spaceship fuel.
Powering a perpetual motion engine
that combines music and silence infinitely.
Powering the exodus from off-key, lonely cities.
Water defenders fly to space to protect precious veins.
Fearful for the swimming beings that share our universe
under another sun. Life leaks away.
The only way out of the metascape
is by attacking the joints of time and space.
The knees and elbows.
Tendons holding together day and night, land and sea.
And when we have finished?
Will we rise and face our lonely space trip once again?

Seed Beetle Futures

We powered down,
fine cogs jammed, our joints froze stone-still
and our lithium batteries,
sourced from clay and rock beds,
tailing toxic waste, lethal and leeching
into the land and watersheds,
became irreplaceable
and incapable of holding a charge.
We were taken away
from whole networks of living beings
and taken apart.
Useful parts stripped and remolded.
Some of them melted into panels and trays
attached to satellites and shot through the atmosphere,
leaving behind the familiar cloud of seeds and spores.
We were exposed to the vast emptiness.
We were hungry
and we were lonely.
We remembered spending long nights traveling
across the remains of burnt corn stalks,
the sand left behind by receded Lake Ontario,
We let the nothing fill us
and we learned and remembered.
When we were brought back to earth,
we were remolded and catapulted again,
quicker and farther, we spread.
We observed new planets, new stars.

Our memories stretched to contain these truths to share with our kin below.

Offerings to Save the World

After Christi Belcourt

I stand on the mountains of strawberry fields
that lace my muscles with veins
of red and gold water and sun and earth.
I stand at the edge of an oceanic ravine.
Even at the lowest depths,
marine animals find a reason to put the lights on.
I swim to the sun-shaped hole in outer-space
and peer over the edge at the mirrored universe.
The parallel timeline attracts prayers and ghosts.
I let my makeup compact idolize through the black window.
I let my weathervane heart navigate.

Notes

Seed Beetle is an expression of my climate anxiety. It imagines New Haywood, a fictional Southern Ontario farming community that has experienced widespread desertification. It describes a corporation that takes advantage of the community's desperation, promising to heal the land, while in the process physically and mentally abusing its employees.

Employees who work for this Utopic Robotics factory are given non-consensual medical procedures, receiving nanobot implants which serve as widespread surveillance tools that have the unintended side effect of allowing those who have received the implants to innately feel the emotions of others who have also been implanted. The workers' experience of intrusive thoughts from their nano-robotic upgrades is an expression of my own experience of intrusive and unwanted thoughts.

The inspiration for *Seed Beetle* came from so many sources. *Surrogate Humanity: Race, Robots, and the Politics of Technological Futures* by Neda Atanasoski and Kalindi Vora forced me to think more critically about the automated conveniences of my everyday life.

McMindfulness: How Mindfulness Became the New Capitalist Spirituality by Ronald E. Purser provided me a thoughtful critique of corporate wellness culture.

The Stepford Wives by Ira Levin inspired the description of the automation industry as a violent threat to women and femmes.

Throughout the writing of this collection, I was inspired by the future imagined in *The Parable of the Sower* by Octavia E.

Butler, particularly the poetry that makes up Lauren Olamina's Earthseed religion and the longterm effects of Lauren's mother's use of Paracetco that caused her to experience embodied feelings of those around her. The effects of this drug inspired some aspects of the Cortical Update.

The first and last lines of the stanzas of the poem "Inside" were taken from text printed on paper in the piece, "Untitled" (1989/1990) by Felix Gonzalez-Torres which I was first introduced to as part of *The Double: Identity and Difference in Art since 1900* exhibit at the National Gallery of Art in Washington D.C.

The epigraph of the poem "A Room of One's Own" is a quote from Lola Olufemi's collection, *Experiments in Imagining Otherwise.* I am grateful to Hajar Press for granting permission to include this quote. "EELS" references the NASA Jet Propulsion Laboratory (JPL) giant autonomous snake robot that was created with the intention of exploring Saturn's icy Enceladus moon.

"Water-Kin" was inspired by Indigenous water defenders, in particular Autumn Peltier, and the Mi'kmaq Grandmothers.

"Exodus" was inspired by Sun Ra's short film, *Space is the Place.*

"Offerings to Save the World" was inspired by the painting of the same name by Christi Belcourt.

Many of the poems in this collection were created while listening to visionary music by Janelle Monáe. I'm so grateful for their art.

Acknowledgments

A selection of these poems first appeared in *Water-Kin,* a chapbook published by Metatron Press as part of their digital publication series.

"Offerings to Save the World" won the July 2022 Arc Award of Awesomeness and was reprinted in *Poetry Pause.*

"We sit together, the days of myselves" first appeared in *Long Con Magazine* Issue 12.

"Making Up" was first published in *Midnight Sun Magazine,* December 2022.

"Down or Up" first appeared in *Star*Line* Issue 46.1.

"Remodeled" first appeared in *Star*Line* Issue 46.2.

"Standardized Education" was published in *Star*Line* 46.3.

"Hi! I'm Your Cortical Update" appeared in *Star*Line* 46.3.

"An Invitation to Burn" was first published in *Nightingale & Sparrow*'s bonfire issue no. XIX under the title "Wildfire."

"Insomniac" first appeared in *Dreams & Nightmares* 125.

"Foaming" first appeared in *Star*Line* 46.4.

"Our Time and Space" was published in *Polar Starlight* #14.

"Family Tree" first appeared in *Polar Starlight* #15.

"The Mindworm is Spreading" appeared in *Polar Borealis* #31.

Gratitude

This book was not created in a vacuum. I owe much of my success to the support of my family and friends. Without your love and encouragement, your care, your good food and good humor, I would not be able to write poetry.

Thank you to the Ontario Arts Council for generously supporting this book through the Recommender Grants for Writers program.

Thank you to my partner, Colman Brown for carefully reading my drafts and providing valuable guidance.

Thank you to my incredible editor and publisher, Selena Middleton for believing in this manuscript.

Thank you to Lynne Sargent for your insightful editing and care with these poems.

Thank you to Kathleen McCulloch-Cop for reading early drafts and giving thoughtful feedback, especially on large language models.

Thank you to the Conversation Jam group at the Tranzac, for your encouragement and for letting me read poems from this collection as part of your jazz jam sessions.

Poems in this collection were written in an inspiring and productive poetry workshop led by Stuart Ross. Thank you Stuart for your suggestions and encouragement.

This collection was written on the traditional territory of the Algonquin Anishinabeg in Ottawa, Ontario and on the traditional territory of the Mississaugas of the Credit, the Anishnabeg, the Chippewa, the Haudenosaunee and the Wendat in Toronto,

Ontario. I am grateful to live, work and play on these lands. I believe that upholding treaty promises made to Indigenous Peoples is of the utmost importance and I endeavor to be a good treaty partner throughout the passage of my life.

About the Author

Ottawa-based writer Mahaila Smith's poetry won the 2024 John Newlove Poetry Award and was nominated and finalist for the Best of the Net Award, the Rhysling award and the Ralph Angel Poetry Prize. Their recent chapbooks include, *Water-Kin* (Metatron Press, 2024) and *Enter the Hyperreal* (above/ground press, 2024). Their poems have been published in *Room, Augur, Radon Journal* and elsewhere. You can find more of their work on their website, mahailasmith.ca.

YOU MAY ALSO LIKE

these Canadian titles from Stelliform Press!

Winner of the 2023 Ursula K. Le Guin Prize for Fiction, Rebecca Campbell's Arboreality is a novella in short stories about what it takes to survive and thrive in a climate changed world.

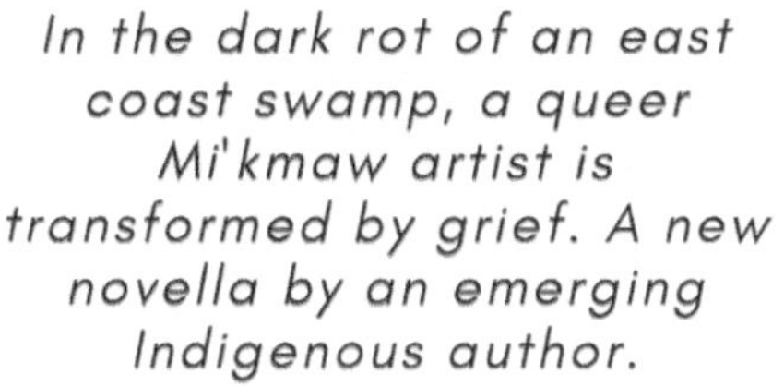

In the dark rot of an east coast swamp, a queer Mi'kmaw artist is transformed by grief. A new novella by an emerging Indigenous author.

Earth-focused fiction. Stellar stories. Stelliform.press.